Weekly Reader Books presents

Published simultaneously in Canada by Holt, Rinehart and Winston of Canada, Limited.

Read With Me is the trademark of Ruth Lerner Perle *Printed in the United States of America*

Library of Congress Cataloging in Publication Data
Horowitz, Susan.
Rumpelstiltskin with Benjy and Bubbles.
(Read with me series)
An adaptation of Rumpelstiltskin.
SUMMARY: A rhymed retelling of the classic tale, with the addition of Benjy the bunny and Bubbles the cat.
[1. Fairy tales. 2. Folklore—Germany. 3. Stories in rhyme] I. Perle, Ruth Lerner, joint author. II. Maestro, Giulio. III. Rumpelstiltskin. IV. Title. V. Series.
PZ8.3.H785Ru [398.2] [E] 78-55628
ISBN 0-03-044956-1
Weekly Reader Books' edition

Rumpelstiltskin
with Benjy and Bubbles

Adapted by SUSAN HOROWITZ
and RUTH LERNER PERLE

Illustrated by GIULIO MAESTRO

Holt, Rinehart and Winston • New York

Once, in a mill by a stream of water,
There lived a Miller and his daughter.
The Miller told tales of great things he could do—
Things that more often than not were untrue.

One day when the Miller was out for a walk,
He encountered the King and they started to talk.
In a voice that was boastful and bragging and bold,
Said the Miller, "My daughter spins straw into gold."

Benjy the bunny heaved a sad sigh;
But Bubbles the cat had a gleam in her eye!

A Miller met the King.
"My daughter can spin straw into gold,"
lied the Miller.

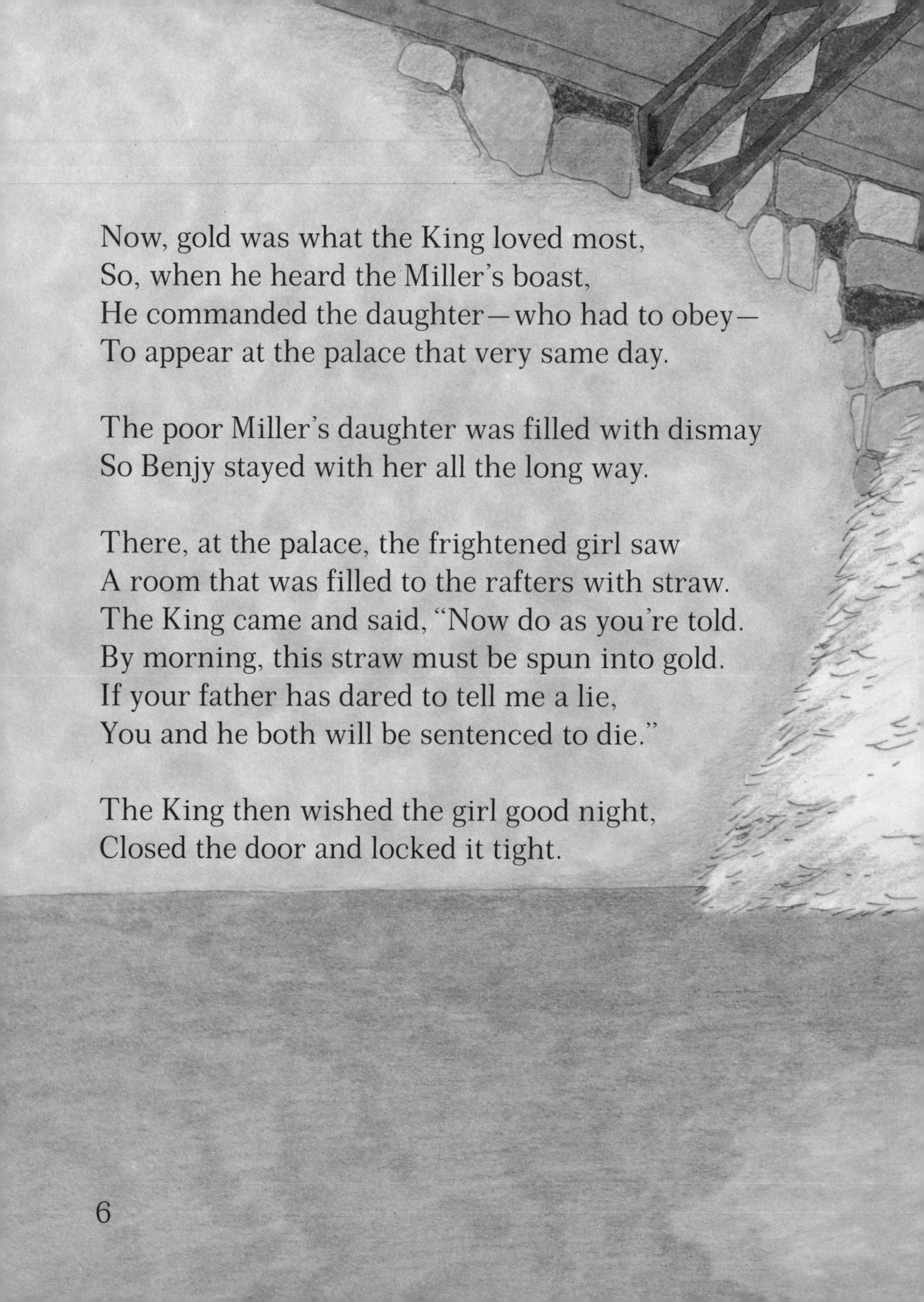

Now, gold was what the King loved most,
So, when he heard the Miller's boast,
He commanded the daughter—who had to obey—
To appear at the palace that very same day.

The poor Miller's daughter was filled with dismay
So Benjy stayed with her all the long way.

There, at the palace, the frightened girl saw
A room that was filled to the rafters with straw.
The King came and said, "Now do as you're told.
By morning, this straw must be spun into gold.
If your father has dared to tell me a lie,
You and he both will be sentenced to die."

The King then wished the girl good night,
Closed the door and locked it tight.

The King sent for the Miller's daughter.
"Spin this straw into gold," said the King.
The girl cried and cried.

The Miller's daughter started to cry
And said, "Benjy, dear bunny, I don't want to die!"
But just at that moment, a strange Elf skipped in,
Followed by Bubbles, who wore a sly grin.
"Good day," said the Elf, "or, rather, good night.
I see that you've had a bit of a fright.
Straw into gold? Is that what it's about?"
"It is!" cried the girl. "And there seems no way out!"

The little Elf smiled, "Oh, I wouldn't say that!"
"And neither would I," meowed Bubbles the cat.

The girl sobbed, "Please help me! I'd give anything!"
"You would?" smirked the Elf, "then let's start with your ring."

So she gave him her ring, still trembling with fright,
And the Elf spun the straw into gold all that night.

A little Elf came.
He said, "Give me your ring.
Then I will spin the straw into gold."
The girl gave her ring.

The little Elf made the straw into gold.
Then he ran away.

When spools of bright gold were piled everywhere,
The Elf and the cat vanished into the air.
And when the sun rose up high in the sky,
The King who loved gold came walking by.

He stared at all the spools of gold—
As many as the room could hold,
Then looked at the girl and whispered in awe,
"I have many more rooms and much more straw.
I want another room of gold!
And you must do as you are told."

Then he showed her to another room
And left her weeping in the gloom.
Benjy, who knew her grief and fears,
Gently licked away her tears.

The King liked the gold.
"You must make more gold,"
he said to the girl.
The girl cried and cried.

When midnight came, just as before,
The magic Elf skipped in the door.

With Benjy the bunny at her side,
The girl fell to her knees and cried,
"Oh, help me meet the King's commands,
And fill these spools with golden strands!"

Said the Elf, "Your father's words were reckless!
But I'll help you if you give me your necklace."

So she gave him her chain with the golden heart locket
And the little Elf pinned it onto his pocket.
Then he took some straw and started to spin,
As Bubbles watched with a mischievous grin.

The Elf came.
He said, "Give me your locket.
Then I will make the gold."
The girl gave her locket.
The Elf made the gold.

By dawn, the whole room seemed to glitter and gleam,
And the little Elf vanished as if in a dream.

The King came and gazed and measured the gold,
Amazed at the treasure the large room could hold.
Then he said, "I can see all the straw has been spun.
This is a fine piece of work you have done.

These riches delight me; I'm thrilled at the sight!
So spin me a room filled with gold one more night.
You'll be my Queen, if you can do it,
And if you don't, you'll surely rue it."
Then he showed her the straw he had heaped in a hall,
One hundred feet wide and one hundred feet tall.

The King then went off to his chambers to sleep,
Leaving the girl and the bunny to weep.

The King said, "Make me gold one more time. Then you may be my Queen."

At midnight, a cloud passed over the moon
As the strange little Elf hopped in whistling a tune.
The girl cried, "I beg you! Please help me to live!"
And the Elf said, "I might—but what will you give?"

"Alas," cried the girl, as she looked about sadly,
"I have nothing to give you and I need you so badly!"
"Oh, you'd be surprised," the little Elf smiled,
"Should you become Queen, you could give me your child!"

The girl said to Benjy, "That might never be."
And Bubbles the cat grinned mischievously.

So the poor Miller's daughter, in a trembling voice,
Said, "I really don't seem to have any choice...
Very well, you may have my first born child."
Then the Elf started spinning the straw and smiled.

The Elf said to the girl, "I will make the gold. When you are Queen, you must give me your child."
The girl said, "Yes."
The Elf made the gold.

By morning, the magical work was all done.
The gold filled the room and shone like the sun.
Then the Elf gave a tug on his little red beard,
And both he and Bubbles the cat disappeared.

As soon as the morning lark rose on its wing,
The big door swung open, and in walked the King.
Since there was more gold than he ever had seen,
The King kept his promise and the girl became Queen.

Then her life was complete with laughter and song,
And a beautiful baby was born before long.

But Benjy the bunny knew something was wrong.

The girl became Queen.
Soon she had a child.

One day, as the Queen strolled out in the sun
With Benjy the bunny and her little one,
The strange little Elf sprang up out of the earth,
And said, "I see there has been a fine, royal birth.
I spun your gold—now, lest you forget—
You owe me a child and must pay your debt."

The Queen begged the Elf to take all her wealth,
Her castle, her kingdom, her beauty, her health.
And she cried, "Oh please, you may take all the rest!
But leave me my child, whom I love the best."

"What I ask," said the Elf, "is my rightful claim.
But I'll give up the child—if you guess my name!"

Then the little Elf vanished—*POOF!*—into the ground,
And the Queen looked about for what names could be found.

The Elf came to take the child.
The Queen cried.
The Elf said, "Guess my name.
Then I will not take the child."

The Queen had her servants make up a great list
So she could be sure that no names would be missed.
There was

Alphonse and Andrew and Amos and Aaron,
Benedict, Brighton, Broderick and Baron,
Hedley and Harold and Horton and Horace,
Milton and Manfred and Morton and Morris,
Philip and Peter and Preston and Paul,
Selwyn and Seymour and Standish and Saul.

The Queen read the names to the Elf the next day,
But after each name, he shook his head—Nay!

Again, the day after, the Queen tried to guess,
But just as before, she had no success.
For each time the Queen named a name that might fit,
The Elf simply snickered and said, "*That's* not it."

At last the Elf said, "You have just one more day!
If you don't guess my name, there's a debt you must pay."

Poor Benjy's heart was filled with pity,
But Bubbles thought the Elf was quite witty.

The Queen could not guess the Elf's name.
Her men made lists of names for her.

Now, the Queen's favorite servant went out in the wood
To find all the names that he possibly could.
He asked every creature that swam, flew or crawled,
But none of them knew what the strange Elf was called.

He walked through the forest to search for himself—
And there, in a cave, he saw the strange Elf!

The Elf and his cat danced all 'round a fire,
And he laughed as he sang, "I have to admire
My wonderful wit, my marvelous mind,
My elegant name which no one can find!
I'm *Rumpelstiltskin!* My name is unique!
And that baby is *mine*!" he cried with a shriek.

A man saw the Elf in the woods.
"My name is Rumpelstiltskin,"
sang the Elf.

The good servant hurried back home to the Queen
And told her about the strange Elf he had seen.
He explained how he saw the Elf dance and exclaim
That Rumpelstiltskin was his real name.

The Queen thanked the servant, and with a great laugh,
She tore the long list of the names right in half.

The man ran to the Queen.
"The Elf's name is Rumpelstiltskin!" he said.

When the Elf came the next day, he gleefully shouted,
"Can you tell me my name? I very much doubt it!"
The Queen frowned as she asked, "Is it David? Or Dwight?"
And the little Elf giggled, "You're not very bright!
The game of my name is over," he smiled.
He stretched out his arms and said, "Give me your child."

"Let me try once again," said the Queen, "then you win."
And she smiled and said sweetly, "You're Rumpelstiltskin!"

The little Elf screamed, "It just isn't fair!"
And then he and the cat vanished into the air.
With them, also vanished all sadness and fears
And the King, Queen and baby were happy for years,
As for Benjy the bunny… he wiggled his ears.

Soon the Elf came for the child.
“Your name is Rumpelstiltskin!”
cried the Queen.
The Elf ran away.
The Queen was happy.

THE END